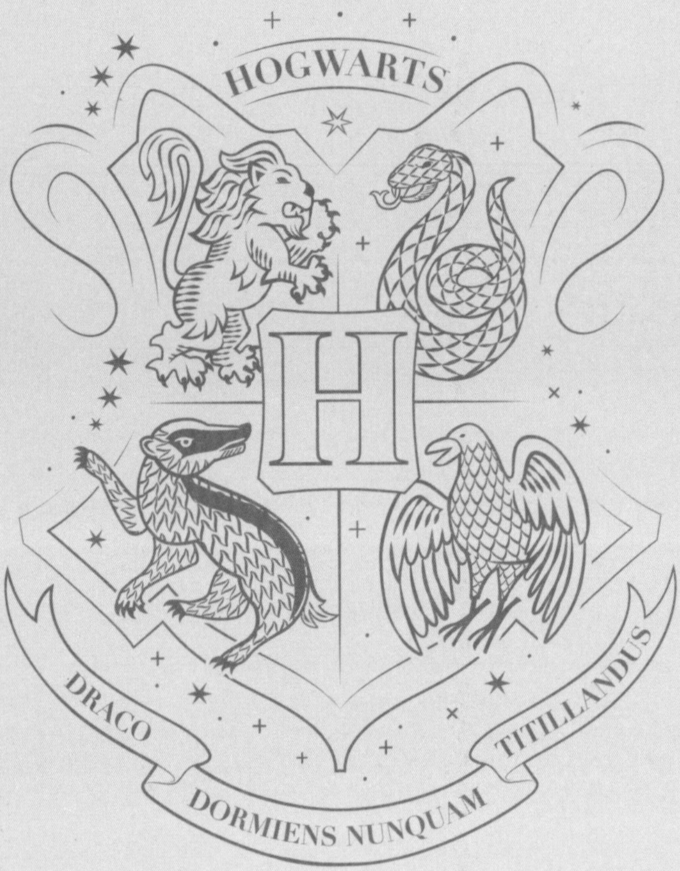

PROPERTY OF:

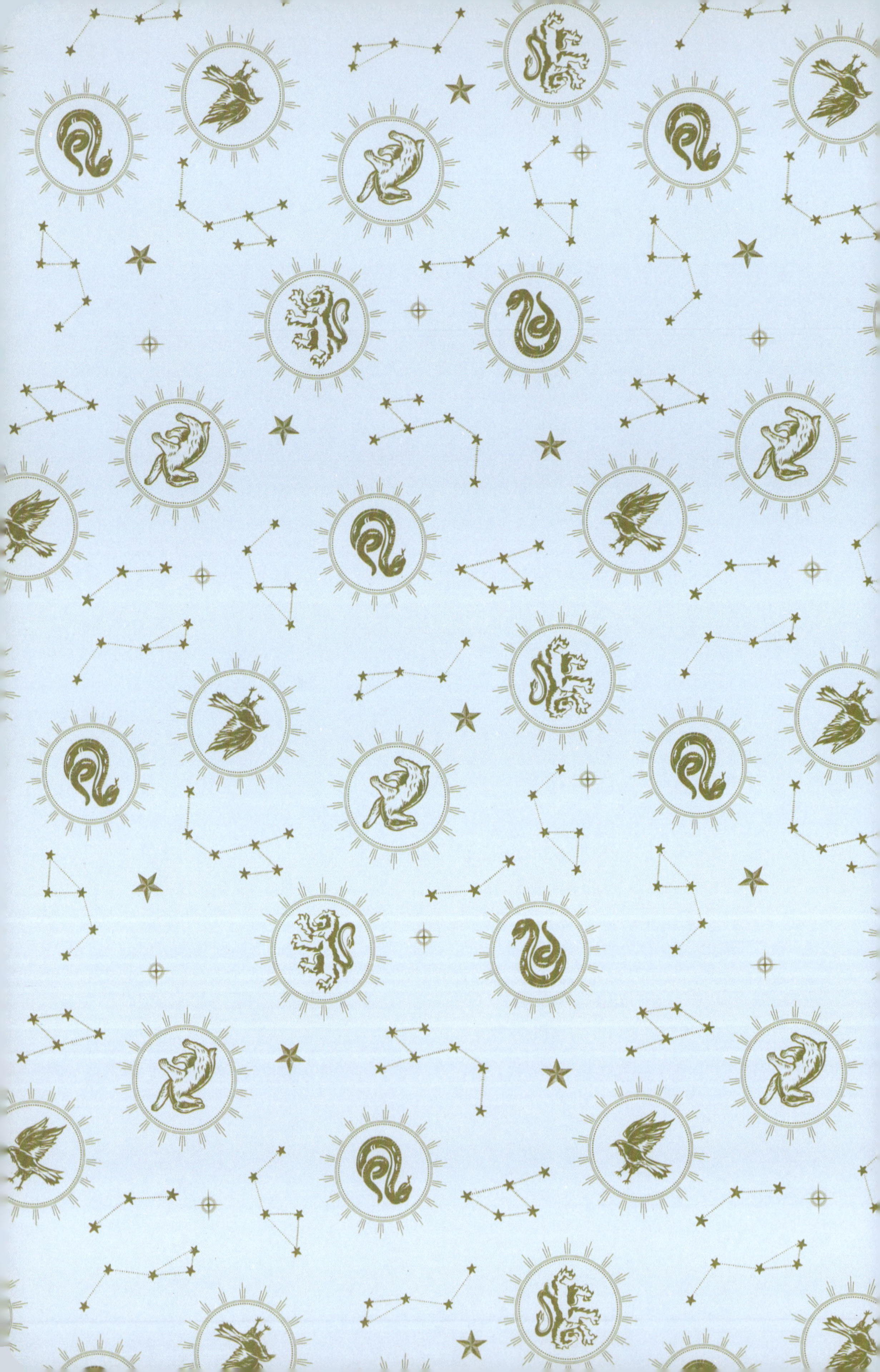

JULY

JULY 2022

SUNDAY	MONDAY	TUESDAY	WEDNESDAY
3	4 Independence Day	5	6
10	11	12	13
17	18	19	20
24 31 Harry Potter's Birthday	25	26	27

JULY 2022

THURSDAY	FRIDAY	SATURDAY	Notes
	1	2	
7	8	9	
14	15	16	
21	22	23	
28	29	30	

JUNE 27–JULY 3

27 Monday

28 Tuesday

29 Wednesday

NOTES

30 Thursday

1 Friday

2 Saturday

3 Sunday

NOTES

JULY 4–10

4 Monday

INDEPENDENCE DAY

5 Tuesday

6 Wednesday

NOTES

JULY 4–10

7 Thursday

8 Friday

9 Saturday

10 Sunday

NOTES

JULY 11–17

11 Monday

12 Tuesday

13 Wednesday

NOTES

JULY 11–17

14 Thursday

15 Friday

16 Saturday

17 Sunday

NOTES

JULY 18–24

18 Monday

19 Tuesday

20 Wednesday

NOTES

21 Thursday

22 Friday

23 Saturday

24 Sunday

NOTES

JULY 25–31

25 Monday

26 Tuesday

27 Wednesday

NOTES

JULY 25–31

28 Thursday

29 Friday

30 Saturday

31 Sunday HARRY POTTER'S BIRTHDAY

NOTES

AUG

AUGUST 2022

SUNDAY	MONDAY	TUESDAY	WEDNESDAY
	1	2	3
7	8	9	10
14	15	16	17
21	22	23	24
28	29 Summer Bank Holiday (UK)	30	31

AUGUST 2022

THURSDAY	FRIDAY	SATURDAY	Notes
4	5	6	
11	12	13	
18	19	20	
25	26	27	

AUGUST 1–7

1 Monday

2 Tuesday

3 Wednesday

NOTES

AUGUST 1–7

4 Thursday

5 Friday

6 Saturday

7 Sunday

NOTES

AUGUST 8–14

8 Monday

9 Tuesday

10 Wednesday

NOTES

11 Thursday

12 Friday

13 Saturday

14 Sunday

NOTES

AUGUST 15–21

15 Monday

16 Tuesday

17 Wednesday

NOTES

AUGUST 15–21

18 Thursday

19 Friday

20 Saturday

21 Sunday

NOTES

AUGUST 22–28

22 Monday

23 Tuesday

24 Wednesday

NOTES

AUGUST 22–28

25 Thursday

26 Friday

27 Saturday

28 Sunday

NOTES

SEPT

SEPTEMBER 2022

SUNDAY	MONDAY	TUESDAY	WEDNESDAY
4	5 Labor Day	6	7
11	12	13	14
18	19 Hermione Granger's Birthday	20	21
25 Rosh Hashanah Begins at Sundown	26	27	28

SEPTEMBER 2022

THURSDAY	FRIDAY	SATURDAY	Notes
	2	3	
	9	10	
	16	17	
	23	24	
	30		

AUGUST 29–SEPTEMBER 4

29 Monday SUMMER BANK HOLIDAY (UK)

30 Tuesday

31 Wednesday

NOTES

AUGUST 29–SEPTEMBER 4

1 Thursday

2 Friday

3 Saturday

4 Sunday

NOTES

SEPTEMBER 5–11

5 Monday LABOR DAY

6 Tuesday

7 Wednesday

NOTES

SEPTEMBER 5–11

8 Thursday

9 Friday

10 Saturday

11 Sunday

NOTES

SEPTEMBER 12–18

12 Monday

13 Tuesday

14 Wednesday

NOTES

SEPTEMBER 12–18

15 Thursday

16 Friday

17 Saturday

18 Sunday

NOTES

SEPTEMBER 19–25

19 Monday

HERMIONE GRANGER'S BIRTHDAY

20 Tuesday

21 Wednesday

NOTES

SEPTEMBER 19–25

22 Thursday

23 Friday

24 Saturday

25 Sunday

ROSH HASHANAH
BEGINS AT SUNDOWN

NOTES

SEPTEMBER 26–OCTOBER 2

26 Monday

27 Tuesday

28 Wednesday

NOTES

SEPTEMBER 26–OCTOBER 2

29 Thursday

30 Friday

1 Saturday

2 Sunday

NOTES

OCT

OCTOBER 2022

SUNDAY	MONDAY	TUESDAY	WEDNESDAY
2	3	4 Yom Kippur Begins at Sundown	5
9	10 Columbus Day Indigenous Peoples' Day	11	12
16	17	18	19
23	24	25	26
30	31 Halloween		

OCTOBER 2022

THURSDAY	FRIDAY	SATURDAY	Notes
		1	
6	7	8	
3	14	15	
0	21	22	
7	28	29	

OCTOBER 3–9

3 Monday

4 Tuesday

YOM KIPPUR BEGINS AT SUNDOWN

5 Wednesday

NOTES

OCTOBER 3–9

6 Thursday

7 Friday

8 Saturday

9 Sunday

NOTES

OCTOBER 10–16

10 Monday

COLUMBUS DAY
INDIGENOUS PEOPLES' DAY

11 Tuesday

12 Wednesday

NOTES

13 Thursday

14 Friday

15 Saturday

16 Sunday

NOTES

OCTOBER 17–23

17 Monday

18 Tuesday

19 Wednesday

NOTES

OCTOBER 17–23

20 Thursday

21 Friday

22 Saturday

23 Sunday

NOTES

OCTOBER 24–30

24 Monday

25 Tuesday

26 Wednesday

NOTES

OCTOBER 24–30

27 Thursday

28 Friday

29 Saturday

30 Sunday

NOTES

NOV

NOVEMBER 2022

SUNDAY	MONDAY	TUESDAY	WEDNESDAY
		1	2
6 Daylight Savings Time Ends	7	8	9
13	14	15	16
20	21	22	23
27	28	29	30

NOVEMBER 2022

THURSDAY	FRIDAY	SATURDAY	Notes
3	4	5	
0	11 Veterans Day	12	
7	18	19	
4 anksgiving Day	25	26	

OCTOBER 31–NOVEMBER 6

31 Monday HALLOWEEN

1 Tuesday

2 Wednesday

NOTES

OCTOBER 31–NOVEMBER 6

3 Thursday

4 Friday

5 Saturday

6 Sunday

DAYLIGHT SAVINGS TIME ENDS

NOTES

NOVEMBER 7–13

7 Monday

8 Tuesday

9 Wednesday

NOTES

NOVEMBER 7–13

10 Thursday

11 Friday

VETERANS DAY

12 Saturday

13 Sunday

NOTES

NOVEMBER 14–20

14 Monday

15 Tuesday

16 Wednesday

NOTES

17 Thursday

18 Friday

19 Saturday

20 Sunday

NOTES

NOVEMBER 21–27

21 Monday

22 Tuesday

23 Wednesday

NOTES

NOVEMBER 21–27

24 Thursday THANKSGIVING DAY

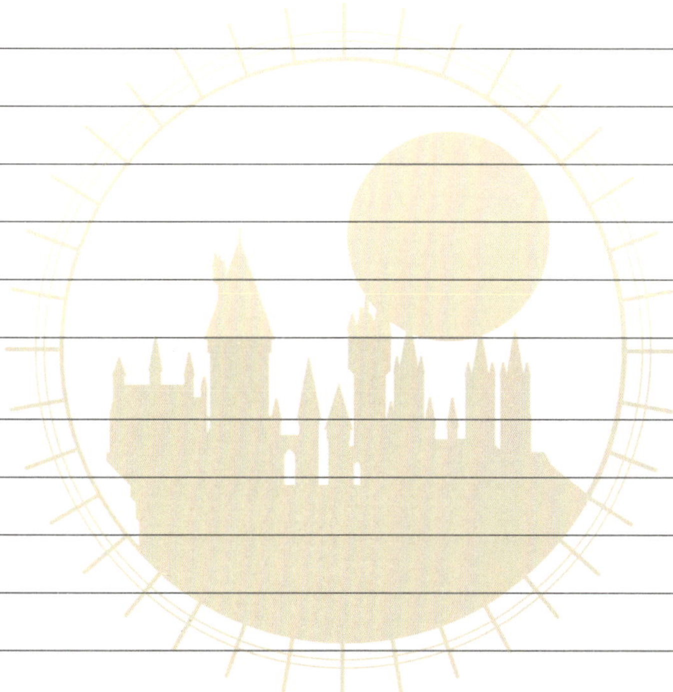

25 Friday

26 Saturday

27 Sunday

NOTES

DEC

DECEMBER 2021

SUNDAY	MONDAY	TUESDAY	WEDNESDAY
4	5	6	7
11	12	13	14
18	19 Hanukkah Begins at Sundown	20	21
25 Christmas Day	26 First Day of Kwanzaa Boxing Day (UK)	27	28

DECEMBER 2021

THURSDAY	FRIDAY	SATURDAY	Notes
1	2	3	
8	9	10	
15	16	17	
22	23	24 Christmas Day Eve	
29	30	31 New Year's Eve	

NOVEMBER 28–DECEMBER 4

28 Monday

29 Tuesday

30 Wednesday

NOTES

NOVEMBER 28–DECEMBER 4

1 Thursday

2 Friday

3 Saturday

4 Sunday

NOTES

DECEMBER 5–11

5 Monday

6 Tuesday

7 Wednesday

NOTES

DECEMBER 5–11

8 Thursday

9 Friday

10 Saturday

11 Sunday

NOTES

DECEMBER 12–18

12 Monday

13 Tuesday

14 Wednesday

NOTES

DECEMBER 12–18

15 Thursday

16 Friday

17 Saturday

18 Sunday

NOTES

DECEMBER 19–25

19 Monday

HANUKKAH BEGINS AT SUNDOWN

20 Tuesday

21 Wednesday

NOTES

DECEMBER 19–25

22 Thursday

23 Friday

24 Saturday — CHRISTMAS DAY EVE

25 Sunday — CHRISTMAS DAY

NOTES

DECEMBER 26–JANUARY 1

26 Monday

FIRST DAY OF KWANZAA
BOXING DAY (UK)

27 Tuesday

28 Wednesday

NOTES

DECEMBER 26–JANUARY 1

29 Thursday

30 Friday

31 Saturday NEW YEAR'S EVE

1 Sunday NEW YEAR'S DAY

NOTES

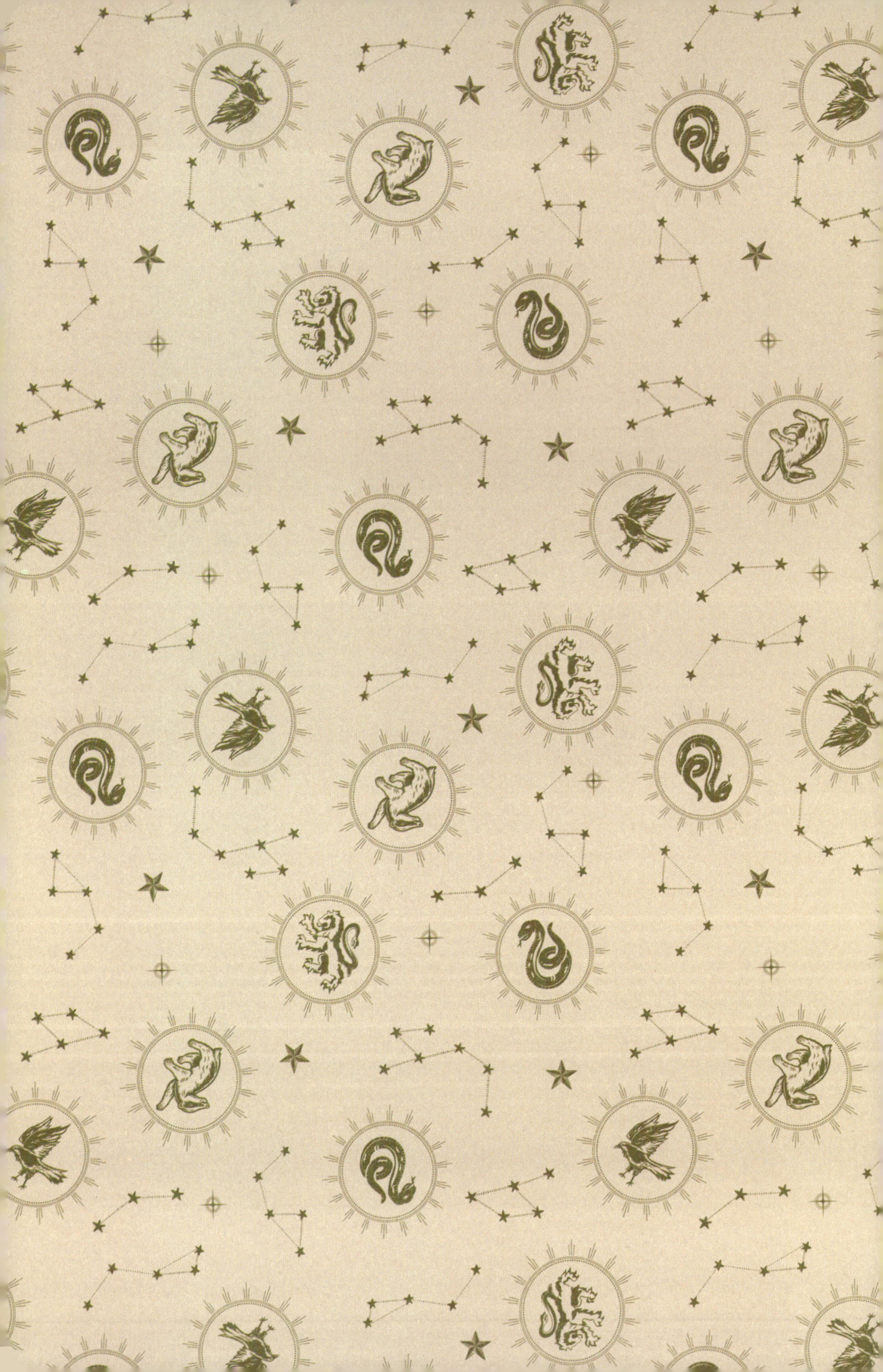

JAN

JANUARY 2023

SUNDAY	MONDAY	TUESDAY	WEDNESDAY
1 New Year's Day	2	3	4
8	9	10	11
15	16 Martin Luther King Jr. Day	17	18
22	23	24	25
29	30	31	

JANUARY 2023

THURSDAY	FRIDAY	SATURDAY	Notes
5	6	7	
2	13	14	
9	20	21	
6	27	28	

JANUARY 2–8

2 Monday

3 Tuesday

4 Wednesday

NOTES

JANUARY 2–8

5 Thursday

6 Friday

7 Saturday

8 Sunday

NOTES

JANUARY 9–15

9 Monday

10 Tuesday

11 Wednesday

NOTES

JANUARY 9–15

12 Thursday

13 Friday

14 Saturday

15 Sunday

NOTES

JANUARY 16–22

16 Monday — MARTIN LUTHER KING JR. DAY

17 Tuesday

18 Wednesday

NOTES

JANUARY 16–22

19 Thursday

20 Friday

21 Saturday

22 Sunday

NOTES

JANUARY 23–29

23 Monday

24 Tuesday

25 Wednesday

NOTES

JANUARY 23–29

26 Thursday

27 Friday

28 Saturday

29 Sunday

NOTES

FEB

FEBRUARY 2023

SUNDAY	MONDAY	TUESDAY	WEDNESDAY
			1
5	6	7	8
12	13	14 Valentine's Day	15
19	20 Presidents' Day	21	22
26	27	28	

FEBRUARY 2023

THURSDAY	FRIDAY	SATURDAY	Notes
2 Groundhog Day	3	4	
9	10	11	
16	17	18	
23	24	25	

JANUARY 30–FEBRUARY 5

30 Monday

31 Tuesday

1 Wednesday

NOTES

JANUARY 30–FEBRUARY 5

2 Thursday

GROUNDHOG DAY

3 Friday

4 Saturday

5 Sunday

NOTES

FEBRUARY 6–12

6 Monday

7 Tuesday

8 Wednesday

NOTES

FEBRUARY 6–12

9 Thursday

10 Friday

11 Saturday

12 Sunday

NOTES

FEBRUARY 13–19

13 Monday

14 Tuesday VALENTINE'S DAY

15 Wednesday

NOTES

FEBRUARY 13–19

16 Thursday

17 Friday

18 Saturday

19 Sunday

NOTES

FEBRUARY 20–26

20 Monday PRESIDENTS' DAY

21 Tuesday

22 Wednesday

NOTES

FEBRUARY 20–26

23 Thursday

24 Friday

25 Saturday

26 Sunday

NOTES

MAR

MARCH 2023

SUNDAY	MONDAY	TUESDAY	WEDNESDAY
			1 Ron Weasley's Birthday
5	6	7	8
12 Daylight Savings Time Begins	13	14	15
19	20	21	22
26	27	28	29

MARCH 2023

THURSDAY	FRIDAY	SATURDAY	Notes
2	3	4	
9	10	11	
6	17 Saint Patrick's Day	18	
3	24	25	
0	31		

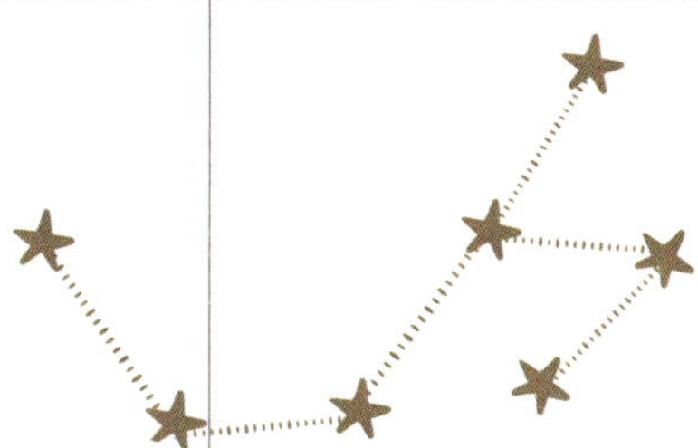

FEBRUARY 27–MARCH 5

27 Monday

28 Tuesday

1 Wednesday RON WEASLEY'S BIRTHDAY

NOTES

FEBRUARY 27–MARCH 5

2 Thursday

3 Friday

4 Saturday

5 Sunday

NOTES

MARCH 6–12

6 Monday

7 Tuesday

8 Wednesday

NOTES

MARCH 6–12

9 Thursday

10 Friday

11 Saturday

12 Sunday

DAYLIGHT SAVINGS TIME BEGINS

NOTES

MARCH 13–19

13 Monday

14 Tuesday

15 Wednesday

NOTES

16 Thursday

17 Friday

SAINT PATRICK'S DAY

18 Saturday

19 Sunday

NOTES

MARCH 20–26

20 Monday

21 Tuesday

22 Wednesday

NOTES

MARCH 20–26

23 Thursday

24 Friday

25 Saturday

26 Sunday

NOTES

MARCH 27–APRIL 2

27 Monday

28 Tuesday

29 Wednesday

NOTES

MARCH 27–APRIL 2

30 Thursday

31 Friday

1 Saturday APRIL FOOLS' DAY

2 Sunday

NOTES

APR

APRIL 2023

SUNDAY	MONDAY	TUESDAY	WEDNESDAY
2	3	4	5 First Day of Passover
9 Easter	10 Easter Monday	11	12
16	17	18	19
23	24	25	26
30			

APRIL 2023

THURSDAY	FRIDAY	SATURDAY	Notes
		1 April Fools' Day	
6	7 Good Friday	8	
3	14	15	
0	21	22 Earth Day	
7	28	29	

APRIL 3–9

3 Monday

4 Tuesday

5 Wednesday FIRST DAY OF PASSOVER

NOTES

APRIL 3–9

6 Thursday

7 Friday GOOD FRIDAY

8 Saturday

9 Sunday EASTER

NOTES

APRIL 10–16

10 Monday EASTER MONDAY

11 Tuesday

12 Wednesday

NOTES

APRIL 10–16

13 Thursday

14 Friday

15 Saturday

16 Sunday

NOTES

APRIL 17–23

17 Monday

18 Tuesday

19 Wednesday

NOTES

20 Thursday

21 Friday

22 Saturday EARTH DAY

23 Sunday

NOTES

APRIL 24–30

24 Monday

25 Tuesday

26 Wednesday

NOTES

APRIL 24–30

27 Thursday

28 Friday

29 Saturday

30 Sunday

NOTES

MAY

MAY 2023

SUNDAY	MONDAY	TUESDAY	WEDNESDAY
	1 Early May Bank Holiday (UK)	2 Anniversary of the Battle of Hogwarts	3
7	8	9	10
14 Mother's Day	15	16	17
21	22	23	24
28	29 Memorial Day Spring Bank Holiday (UK)	30	31

MAY 2023

THURSDAY	FRIDAY	SATURDAY	Notes
4	5	6	
11	12	13	
18	19	20	
25	26	27	

MAY 1–7

1 Monday EARLY MAY BANK HOLIDAY (UK)

2 Tuesday ANNIVERSARY OF THE BATTLE OF HOGWARTS

3 Wednesday

NOTES

4 Thursday

5 Friday

6 Saturday

7 Sunday

NOTES

MAY 8–14

8 Monday

9 Tuesday

10 Wednesday

NOTES

11 Thursday

12 Friday

13 Saturday

14 Sunday MOTHER'S DAY

NOTES

MAY 15–21

15 Monday

16 Tuesday

17 Wednesday

NOTES

MAY 15–21

18 Thursday

19 Friday

20 Saturday

21 Sunday

NOTES

MAY 22–28

22 Monday

23 Tuesday

24 Wednesday

NOTES

25 Thursday

26 Friday

27 Saturday

28 Sunday

NOTES

JUNE

JUNE 2023

SUNDAY	MONDAY	TUESDAY	WEDNESDA
4	5	6	7
11	12	13	14
18 Father's Day	19 Juneteenth	20	21
25	26	27	28

JUNE 2023

THURSDAY	FRIDAY	SATURDAY	Notes
1	2	3	
8	9	10	
15	16	17	
22	23	24	
29	30		

MAY 29–JUNE 4

29 Monday

MEMORIAL DAY
SPRING BANK HOLIDAY (UK)

30 Tuesday

31 Wednesday

NOTES

MAY 29–JUNE 4

1 Thursday

2 Friday

3 Saturday

4 Sunday

NOTES

JUNE 5–11

5 Monday

6 Tuesday

7 Wednesday

NOTES

JUNE 5–11

8 Thursday

9 Friday

10 Saturday

11 Sunday

NOTES

JUNE 12–18

12 Monday

13 Tuesday

14 Wednesday

NOTES

15 Thursday

16 Friday

17 Saturday

18 Sunday FATHER'S DAY

NOTES

JUNE 19–25

19 Monday JUNETEENTH

20 Tuesday

21 Wednesday

NOTES

22 Thursday

23 Friday

24 Saturday

25 Sunday

NOTES

JUNE 26–JULY 2

26 Monday

27 Tuesday

28 Wednesday

NOTES

JUNE 26–JULY 2

29 Thursday

30 Friday

1 Saturday

2 Sunday

NOTES

NOTES

NOTES

NOTES

NOTES

NOTES

Harry Potter

INSIGHTS
an imprint of
INSIGHT EDITIONS
www.insighteditions.com

MANUFACTURED IN CHINA
10 9 8 7 6 5 4 3 2 1